IT WILL BE CC

António Cantiro

ANTÓNIO CANTEIRO

It Will Be Cold
In The Afternoon

eglantyne books

Published by Eglantyne Books ltd,
The Club Room, Conway Hall, 25 Red Lion Square, London
WC1R 4RL.
www.eglantynebooks.com
©2022 Eglantyne Books
ISBN 978-1-913378-09-7
Printed in the UK by Imprint Academic Ltd;
Seychelles Farm, Upton Pyne, Exeter, Devon EX5 5HY,
ImprintDigital.com
A CIP record for this title is available from the British Library.

Book layout and design by Eric Wright
Production team:
Robert and Olivia Temple, Michael Lee, and Eric Wright

PUBLISHER'S NOTE

The publishers wish to thank Dr. Joanna Popielska-Grzbowska for discovering this work in Lello's Bookshop in Porto and recommending it for translation and publication in English. She writes:

'For me it was as if the whole of Portugal of the times of António Nobre and António Canteiro were compressed in an enchanted manner into one small book. The author confided in me that the book *Só (Alone)*, a collection of poems by António Nobre (1867-1900), accompanied him during the years of his academic studies in Coimbra, and later when he attended the Conservatory of Music in Coimbra. During the years 1984-1989 Canteiro kept the book on his bedside table in his attic room as a music student. He played second flute with the Classical Orchestra of Coimbra in sixteen concerts in Portugal, Paris, the Royal Palace in Madrid, and at the European Parliament in Strasbourg. He was born and lives in the municipality of Cantanhede, district of Coimbra. Canteiro says that *It Will Be Cold in the Afternoon* is a biographical book in which the two Antónios meet, both of them students at Coimbra, both lovers of poetry, and of the rustic people of Gândara, and of trips along the Estrada da Beira in search of a beloved. Therefore, this book is an encounter with António Nobre more than a hundred years after his death, and is a tribute paid by one poet to another.'

To my children, students of Coimbra

Here the poet lived the golden days of his Dream
And thus Anto named the slender Tower
Legend of Lonely Soul and mournful heart
Which anointed poets in the favour of his weeping.

ANTÓNIO NOBRE

Caveat

The words in italics in the present narrative were written by the poet António Nobre (1867-1900).

ITINERARY OF THE POET

1867

Santa Catarina Street — Porto (15) Seixo — Entre Douro e Minho (19) Leça da Palmeira — Porto (22) Boa Nova — Leça (25) Penedo da Saudade — Coimbra (30) Almedina Arch — Coimbra (33) Tower of Anto — Coimbra (35).

1988

Quebra Costas — Coimbra (41) Sá da Bandeira Avenue (43) University Courtyard — Coimbra (45) República Square 1 — Coimbra (49) República Square 2 — Coimbra (54) Gala Street — Coimbra — (56) University Tower 1 — Coimbra (59) University Tower 2 — Coimbra (61) Old Square — Coimbra (63) Quinta das Lágrimas — Coimbra (66) Sub Ripas Street — Coimbra (68) Baixinha — Coimbra (70) Porta-Férrea — Coimbra (73) Santa Clara — Coimbra (76).

1889

Carqueja Alley — Coimbra (81) Lixa — Felgueiras (84) Rue Racine — Paris (86) Rue des Écoles — Paris (89) Rue de La Valette — Paris (93) Casais — Penafiel (99) Funchal – Madeira (101) Claravel — Davos (105) Cascais and Monte Estoril — Lisboa (107) Carreiros — Foz do Douro (109).

1867

SANTA CATARINA STREET - PORTO

I

I dreamt of being born (*on a Tuesday, a bell was ringing!*); I came into the world on an August night... what's happening! No ground for these unbalanced feet, the opposite of falling into the water, as if, suddenly, I can feel myself fading away at the bottom of a well, irretrievably falling, running out of breath, with all the surrounding air taking hold of me, filling the inner recesses of my body; completely naked, the cold caressing my skin, a gentle, strange wind, and, overwhelmed by a breath, I begin to cry... along with the bell, there was a scream!...

II

There you go, that is what it is to be born! A shock, a groan, a scream... and that's it, the midwife said.

III

I felt hands picking me up like a shell in the middle of their palms, me, hardly yet a person, red, ensanguined, with a knot of rope tied to my navel; and the stork, outside, flying away in the moonlight from the window; five o'clock in the morning, here, inside, a hot summer day rising, and with it, a baby boy lying beneath the shade of breasts and tears, drops falling endlessly...

IV

Nights went by, days arrived, and today the mother is sitting on the bench of the parlour, balancing the tears on her eyelids, sewing the woollen socks; she threaded the needle, peering into the sunlight that came in through the window; first, she softened the thread in her moist lips, then she repeated the gesture with the help of her fingers, her forefinger and thumb, together; shredding the thread through the hole, she stretched it and cut it with her teeth; the mother gently uttered: José!, where's the sun that was there just now, at the window?, Ana, little do we know of the mystery of the sun, and of time, which sometimes exists, sometimes runs away; the mother reiterated: ah!... and your children, where are they?; to which the father answered: we know little about them, as little as we know about ourselves; José, there's not even a pain that I can call my own, but my body burns in flames, my skin and arms are itching!; you are sick, woman!, you're sweating from the cold, there's a spectre of death in you!; outside in the street, for a moment, the dust of the road was shaken by the wind and, within seconds, the sky melted into a strong rainstorm.

V

Let me go back to your womb, mother! Living every minute inside your wet body, mother! You know about the sea, and the corals, and the starfish, and the whelks, and the moonlight, mother. I remember that one day you said: *I'm going there, to the Grave, António, and I'll be right back*, but to this day you haven't returned! Why, Mother? Do you still want me to return to your womb? Now and at the hour of death?, Amen

VI

Aunt Delfina, such a pure old lady, used to sleep next to me and was always praying... The bells announced the novena, church bells ringing in the evening, and under the shade of the cliffs I laid my tears down; I listened to the sound of the sea in the trees, soft with peace, soft in the stillness of the crags under the willow branches; long canes of sun penetrate the frame of the open window, and dispel the afternoon, leaving me alone, with just the lament of the sea, in the earth's dam, around the cove, and the willow bent by the wind over the wall, covered with the mantle of shade; two dogs barked outside, when... suddenly it thundered; the lightning illuminated the darkness, and Augusto, larger than me, adjusted my body to his, on a chair, extended his arms over my shoulder to calm me down; because I had slept all night revolving around dreams, screaming... and the next day, my brother Augusto approached me with his hands sunk in his trouser pockets, uttering: calm down, it's over! don't put on a sad face, a sick face! And with his wide hand, leaning on the tabletop, he urged me to go play in the street: António, I know how tall your soul is, it is certainly too large for this sky...

SEIXO – ENTRE O DOURO E MINHO

I

I remember crossing the school playground piggy-backing on another boy's back and the teacher hitting me with a wooden ruler on my bum; I gritted my teeth and drew my lips into my mouth, but didn't cry in front of my schoolmates; and at night, sitting at the table, I peeked inside the transparency of the glass of water at my wet eyes and the teacher's fierce face... distracted from myself, I knocked the glass of water over the tablecloth with my elbow; I went to sleep and, in bed, I covered myself with the sheet over my head, so as not to see my wet eyes of passion and the teacher's face filled with rage, hitting me; and, to get away from bad thoughts, I dreamed of the beach and of a wave bouncing on the sand, coming to nestle beside me...

II

Your mended verses may be "Dispersed", Eduardo[1], sewn into the shade of the trees, in the middle of the mountain dust, take them with you when you move to a different home, my friend, or else wait for me to read them to you by the sepulchre of a young boy, which is your grave; your unique childhood, which is my childhood, is in your first verses, the revelation of poets, promises of mysteries, from which my life and yours arose, restless; it is said of my eyes, enormous, immense when they brood, and that I will be *the prince of the poets of my time*, but I leave to you the laurels of fame, if you still have time left to live... My brother, Augusto, says that I am a reserved speaking animal, that I devour books in the nooks around the house, that I always carry Byron under my arm; since my school days, while my chest holds words being born, I feel them fermenting in a tank, itching to see the light, while I sleep (as if it were possible to sleep!), I have a virus gnawing in my body, because only the body leads us to

---

1   TN – A reference to the poetic work of Eduardo Coimbra (1867- 1884), a close friend of António Nobre's.

words, the moving of the hands around, the pointed pen scratching the paper, I repeat: only the body leads us to words, the body and the mind... sometimes I get up from bed and come to the living room, abruptly, I open drawers and close drawers, I look for paper, nibs, ink, and, in a gush, the text runs through the brain to establish itself in letters and written words; I, António, look for my double, the other of me, and I don't find him, like olive oil in water, floating in bubbles, in the enamel basin; *My first verses are in the churchyard, still, written on the lime trees...* I go home reciting this sentence from a poem; I leave home reciting another sentence from another poem; would this also be a way of praying? Just like a sea that hits the rock incessantly, I find myself thinking about the strange way the brave waves rise up in the sea, sprawl on the shore, and lie rolled up in the sand...

III

At night, I listen to my steps in the hallway, I yearn for what was left unsaid; I lie down, I get up, I lie down, I get up, I lie down, I stand up and sit down; in short, I don't want to lose the last word, the one that was left waiting to be said, to be written; it's been hours since I've thought about anything except writing words; it's been minutes since I watched and reviewed the whole city from the window; it's been seconds since dozens of words passed in front of me, I've kept only a few, that I write down, the ones that I don't write and were lost, I don't know where they went; I don't know where the words come from...

IT WILL BE COLD IN THE AFTERNOON

Leça da Palmeira – Porto

I

Who writes in me? It is not me, it's another António in me who puts together letters into syllables, syllables into words, sounds, music... words are a sometimes violent evil that seizes us, that lives in us, an indomitable vice that never wears off; when we walk around with a book, a notebook and a pencil, we walk together with poets, in the company of poets, who write in us; do you write in me, Shakespeare? When I read you and forget you, at some point, I write, and thus I exist!

II

Then I recollect childhood and the ox carts with their wheels rattling on the cobblestone; *the wind moans, the sea roars*, and the Moon, his lover, comes to lie down, in the background, at the tangible limit of the horizon...

III

There are sheep stifled by the clouds all around them, a furry dog stretched out surrounded by clouds; women with black shawls surrounded by clouds, they have in their hands a distaff with giant yarns while clouds swirl around; and broad-shouldered men with cigarettes in the corner of their lips, throwing smoke into the surrounding clouds, they notice the shade of their seared hands, and look at the nets of clouds, to cast them into the sea and into the sky. ... a shepherd, with a cane, shepherds, a flock of lamb-clouds; there is a boy on his way to school with a bag on his arm, stretched out beside his thigh, and an old lady holding him with an arm on his shoulder; at the same time, the old lady is keeping count of the beads of a rosary, praying: Our Father who art in heaven, hallowed be Thy name...

IV

I, António, my own double and alter ego, look into my eyes and brood, in the unique solitude of being alone with myself, accompanying myself with me, which is the other and myself, the two in one, both at the same time, the metamorphosis of myself and the other; being natural and physical; being poetic, mythical, in the same body, two brothers of the same spirit; a dandy and a memory of myself; a natural vocation for the art of writing, through the voice, through the instinct of the search for the last word; music and sound live off letters, together, words made up of reading, of severe self-criticism, even, and, despite the broken heart, there is a sense of orientation towards the cartography of the sound of words and of life...

V

What have you been up to, António, you seem to have vanished?, Augusto inquired, at the table, at suppertime; I answered that I had gone to see the river walking towards the sea, it was crazy, that river, small, narrow, of fresh water, unbridled, about to drown in the salt water, the immense salt water of the ocean; António!, my brother replied, do you know what the salt water is made of in the sea?; I replied with the innocent face of a child, hesitant and doubtful: well... I'm not sure... but I suspect it is made of the tears of the fishermen's widows...

Boa Nova – Leça

I

I was walking on the beach at sunset, right on the surf, with my naked feet, stepping on the seaweed (ah!, such a mild scent of the sea breeze!); I would bend my body to pick up a round shell from the sand, and the next moment I would throw it into the sea, I wanted to see it almost touching the surface of the waters, like a discobolus of an Olympiad, I wanted to see it overcome time beyond this solitude, returning to the sea what belongs to the sea… and I would follow with my eyes the round shell, gliding in the air, the whitish shell that was thrown by my arm's strength, forming a half circle, falling, and then rising, to make yet another half circle, beyond, falling, and again another half circle, then, diving, finally, exhausted, the shell immersing itself in the dark depth of the waters. A shell, into which the whole world can fit, that flat, whitish handful of concave stone, where the land and the sea can fit (ah! a hint in the mouth of the taste of the beach sand); I place my hands on my face and temples, my fingertips on my eyes, on a wrinkle in a valley where the morning sun can fit, wrapped in fog; while I linger, with my eyes half-open, I can hear the seagulls cawing; no one can appease a man, when he has at arm's length, at finger's length, the taste of the salty land, in tears or in sea water hidden in a hand cupped like a shell.

II

When there are fewer people on the beach, mostly only fishermen, mostly only seagulls, mostly only sand, mostly only rocks, mostly only fog, mostly only a dog walking with a beggar on the leash, when there is no one to notice, no one to see that I exist, I bend down and crawl into a burrow in a rock, between the sand, the rocks, close to a chapel, on the other side of the cliff; I look at its front and see a small fragment of stone that I want to describe in my mind down to the last letter, down to the last word, to the end, without suspension points, down to the end, full stop.

III

António would not wear a worn out coat over a worn out white shirt, threadbare collars over the threadbare coat; he would not put on black khaki trousers, with the narrow legs running away from his feet, old quarrels that the felt socks did not hide; António was impressive due to his posture, his bizarre dress, similar to the sepia portrait on the frame in the living room, above the dresser; when he walked, with his hands in his pockets, a hermit's cane in front of his feet, constantly wobbling, he would look at the peak of solitude on the walls, he would see through the window the afternoon and the city leaning over the sea. He was a tall boy, his hair black, curly, his black eyes, his angular face, where his thin lips would sit like an accent over the Spanish n; when he recited verses, his voice would change its tone, emerging as if from a cave on the other side of the world, with his mouth slightly twisted, in a proudly subtle smile, accentuating the words, with his lips emphasising its poetic underlining, flowering the sense of the syllables, the penetrating sound, and at the same time the candour of tamed language, so simple and so unusual.

IV

I open the window's shutters and the warm afternoon glow flashes in front of my eyes; there are women carved on the pavement, little Englishwomen walk by and spin their umbrellas, waving their fans on their cheeks; men, amazed at such a sight, take their hats off their heads and bow, and then toss them back on their heads again; the tide falls, along with the algae, and I can feel the smell of humus on the soil; I open the front door and courageously walk towards the beach, with a book under my arm. On my face a fine beard is growing, soft as turtledove feathers; opening my shirt on my chest, I release shy words in the heat of the evening: the threshing floor of the sea ploughs the dream and the singing, the lulling bell, the sand, the stone, the shade, the stem, the halo of time; were it not for the wind battering the skin between the earth, the threshing floor of the sea drooling with foam, the wind blowing the salty mist of the night, in drops raised high up, like miller's flour, from a windmill with puffed sails turning around and around... then, the flour, buried like seeds in the salt water... It is almost night time on the sea bed, of wrinkled shadows and rocks on the sand, shreds of seagulls in mid-flight; in the shell of the sky, there is a segment of the Moon, blurred, the hull bitten by algae; under the morning profile, on the skin line, the hillock of sand on the body soaked by the murmur of the whelks and corals hidden in the mud.

V

The train arrives at S. Bento and roars, throwing a puff of smoke from its back; people flock in a hurry, crushing one another and raising their luggage above the aisles; they sit in rows of two; minutes later, António is serenely staring at the notebook in front of him, and, sitting down, he thinks... the permanent pen of Anto, the avatar, the other one... the fever of António's poetry, the disease of the letters and the words of the other, the infection of the verses in the mouth; who can actually write the last word? He wants to be alone and he cannot be alone... Today, for the second time, António walks through the city with his eyes fixed on the clarity of the window...

VI

The whistle was heard, announcing the beginning of the march: clickety-clack... clickety-clack... clickety-clack... faster and faster; now, a sudden silence was unheard from the people curled up to each other, seated, or settled in the compartments, on their luggage, or standing; without the slightest sound, their heads held high, watching the heads of the others rising at the end of the corridor, sometimes moving backwards and sometimes moving forwards, at the same pace as the train that speeds up, until they finally sit down in their seats, while the train, a long, disinterested, gasping beast, undertook its march towards Coimbra.

1988

PENEDO DA SAUDADE – COIMBRA

I

There is disappointment in people's faces, whether in those who walk down the street or those who walk up the street (with the lights still on at the top of the lamp posts, the faint glare falling on people's faces), it's not that the disappointment in everyone's eyes has come from the night, but rather from the end of the day, it's not that it arose from some kind of sorrow, but rather from the tedious Sunday afternoon-night routine, when I dragged my suitcase crammed with clothes, the shoes rattling on the pavement, on the steps of some staircase, on the narrow walls of some street, and, for that matter, on a cobblestone road where the unprepared feet dance in a balance of ankle bones; now I am jerkily walking on the Corpo de Deus[1] street, always going upwards, where the women, wearing aprons and lace blouses, lean on the windowsills, with their plentiful, boisterous bosoms, their arms folded across, their grey hair on their wrinkled faces; they who were walking there, decanting their longing from their eyes, serenading in their memory the agony of the days.

II

I was walking by, I said good afternoon, and then I stood there listening to the women; I came in sighing with a tired voice, as I trembled along the way, and I turned my face in amazement at the women's prompt response: Bless your heart!, What a handsome boy that is now arriving! Good to see you!... In the meantime, I asked if they could point me in the direction of Penedo da Saudade, for I had lifted my head above the wall, confirming that that was not the name of the street where I was going to be living; no! Dona Rosalina, the sister of Dona Angélica (two old sisters who live in the same house), interrupted, oh sis (she said with a weary look) it is quicker to go this way... and then turning towards me, she explained, sighing: look, you will only reach Penedo da Saudade after passing the University, the Saint Sebastian

---

1 TN – Corpo de Deus is the Portuguese phrase for the religious feast of Corpus Christi.

Arches, the Avenue and, at the end, you'll find Penedo da Saudade on the left; I followed her explanation of gestures and voice, with my eyes fixed, and the sister sat there sadly nodding (disheartened, apparently tired of life). Finally, thanking them both, I carried on: I went up and down the curved street, I went up and down a straight street again, further on I came across the wide University courtyard, and then, as I descended, I walked through the Arches, into the garden, always walking along the pavement of the Avenue, to the end, I turned left, entering the street of Penedo da Saudade; as I approached, I looked at the sign and confirmed that it was right there; daring, calmer now, I looked for the door number, then I entered, opening it and then closing it behind me; I came in with my bulging suitcase, the newspaper stuck under my arm; as soon as I came upon the mirror of the living room, I looked to my side and, turning around, I threw the weekly newspaper contemptuously on the table, and the suitcase, exhausted by the journey, was thrown upon the bed. I heard the door slamming shut, and the pine stairs creaking at every step as I climbed them.

III

As we have seen, António entered the house and closed the door of the sad bedroom, António turned on the light of the equally sad hallway, after turning off the bulb that illuminates the stairs, he turned on the light of the bedroom, after turning off the light of the hallway and sticking the umbrella in the cloakroom hidden behind the entrance door; Dona Carlota, with her hands crossed behind her back, at the end of the stairs, shouted: Have you arrived yet, young man?, Yes, at last I've arrived! A fortuitous flash of lightning lit up his room, a part of the hallway and a crack of the stairs; a vacuum of fear and solitude sounded in António's chest, in that inexplicable Sunday afternoon-night emptiness; at the end of the stairs he could hear Dona Carlota, almost on the run, disappearing: the face of today's weather shows that tomorrow it will rain!... maybe it will!... or maybe it won't!... good night...

ARCO DE ALMEDINA – COIMBRA

I

It was late morning when I opened the window to the sun; the steam from the shower, trapped in the cubicle, snaked through the window guard and disappeared into the open air, free; then, sitting at the table, slowly scalding my mouth and tongue, I drank the milk, chewed the bowl of bread soup and, finally, after standing up, had a thoughtful coffee; when I brushed my teeth in front of the mirror, after scratching my chin, I postponed the shaving of my thin beard for later; I said see you later to Dona Carlota and went out into the street, closing the door behind me; while walking on the pavement, I pressed my lips, my tongue nailed to the palate, trying to keep inside, and for a long time, the aroma of Dona Carlota's hot coffee... Dona Carlota, whose message I still heard, on my way out, in a shaky voice: young man, put on some warm clothes, it is cold!, Dona Carlota, who permanently chews her toothless chops, repeated (now in my ears, in an echo): look, young man, put on some warm clothes, it's cold!, Dona Carlota who placed the coat on my back, as if I were her son, and who repeated what she had repeated again (in my brain, grinding): look, young man, put on some warm clothes, it's cold! I still heard the echo of Dona Carlota's voice (and it's been ten minutes since I got to the street), repeating advice that she always gave: *my handsome boy, may Our Lady make you happy*; turning a corner, I jumped to the other side of the street, to the left, and that voice insisted (the mouth chewing, tasting): the young man!, crossing the street, you can't be careful enough!... and then, in another murmur, almost in silence: *my handsome boy, may Our Lady make you happy.*

II

Around the end of yet another street, to the top, then to the right, through the narrow access, I plunged into the Almedina Arch, slowed down my step and climbed the staircase of the Quebra-Costas, that leads to the Alta; I counted the steps going up: one, two, three, four... ninety-one, if I'm not mistaken; I stood on another flight of stairs, sat down on the last step before the cobblestone square, gained the courage to climb the narrow street that leads to the historic centre, to the Old Cathedral, the cobblestone with several entrances and exits, depending on whether one is coming or going...

TOWER OF ANTO – COIMBRA

I

Looking from above, I see the Mondego river, imprisoned between the houses and the Tower of Anto; I peek at the river, in the background, I see it from the long, narrow window; the afternoon falls on the curves of the wall, on the ochre stone texture, on the grooves and veins between the rectangular blocks (thirty centimetres long, twenty centimetres high and wide) lying on top of each other; there are shadows moving inside the walls, inside the Tower, where echoes persist, and have lived since time immemorial; I raise my eyes to the window and invoke the nymphs (Helen, Porcy, and Charlotte) for the infinite drama of the Moon, *your bride - incarcerated,* I also tell Cândida Ramos, at the Hotel Estefânia, to sit next to me, all of them, dressed with the veil of this light, a coarse light, the moonlight of this night, and to be the sea breeze and the inspiration, the murmur that will whisper in my ear the right words, the only words to write a poem... and also to you, *my chaste Ptolemy in skirts, geometer of the sky!,* spills the trickle of olive oil, of life, which will lead me to death, *on a Friday of passion;* keep away from me this uneducated youth of the present, wandering through the streets of the city, with cloaks and cassocks waving in the wind, ominous ravens from a medieval past that no longer exists; instead of the *praxe*[1], bring to me the pilgrimages of a different time, the sound of bells in the village, the group walks for the nights of novena, the wandering in the fields where the breeze caresses the greenery; and you, miserable one!, you saw at least that life is the greatest enemy of beauty, for while the first lasts too long, the other does not cease until it is over; you don't belong to this world, you only spend a few months here, years, not many, perhaps because of that, allow us both to go outside singing along the street arm in arm, allow the poet to climb the Tower of his Anto and, in the solitude of his singing, an avatar of himself, to sip the waters of the Mondego drop by drop, in the background,

---

1 TN – Praxe is the Portuguese word for the initiation rituals, or 'hazing', that many older students subject freshmen to in some Portuguese universities. Anthos is Ancient Greek for 'flower'.

the same waters that one day will fall from his eyes in tears, when the Sun ceases to be seen and the Moon stubbornly hides behind the clouds...

II

I have settled in the Tower of Anto the writing workshop, my creative sanctuary, the place chosen for the epiphany of verses; I am searching for myself, because I have lost myself on an infinite path, on a path of almost absolute, almost definitive search, longing for a dream: I want to attain possession, in this house of words, which was once the Tower of Babel... *In the Tower of Anto where I live!, there enclosed in a hole, smoke, and, while smoking, sometimes I... weep*; the Tower of António, of Anto, the name born in Ancient Greece, which is said to be the flower, the *anthos* of my garden, the fragrant flower in which I lie, the blood of my blood, the intoxicating odour which amazes and thrills me...

III

The colour of the fruits in the orange grove is that of the Sun-set, the oranges are so juicy that it hurts in the chest to see them dripping down the wall (the wall, outside, on the walkway that connects to the Tower); the oranges crushed into drops, in the flower of the wall, are the tears on the wall, mixed in the bewitched laughter of children...

IV

I get up, I leave home and I want to take you with me, walk hand in hand; but before I go any further, I want to give you words more than flowers, draw smiles more than promises from your lips, throw from the top of the tower (this which was once the Tower of the Prior of Ameal, the part of the medieval walls of the city, following from here towards the slope) a branch of words as beautiful as roses at you, wrapped in smiles, send you from this part overlooking the Mondego, the river of water that we see, serene, flowing in the background...

1988

QUEBRA-COSTAS – COIMBRA

I

Here, between step seventy and step eighty, in Quebra-Costas, if we turn left, we'll be two steps away from the house where the poet lived a century ago; it is a narrow street, crowded with old houses, embedded in high walls, on one side and on the other, walls plastered in white until the ancient roofs which, seen from the ground, seem to bow to our passage; the stonework of the windows has wrinkles and the winding granite path shows us in the background the arch of the ancient city wall, the ochre, sturdy wall, sneaking to the left, leading us to António's creative sanctuary; still going up, leaving behind the Tower of Anto, the tower with narrow windows open to the river, if we curve to the right and descend diagonally, we find the cobbled street that goes down to the toll; going up to the side of the Old Cathedral, on the left, along the street in front, we come across the Machado de Castro museum, and, on top, on the right, the University; if we instead walk on the opposite side, following the Old Cathedral, straight ahead, along a narrow street, we see the University; in short, and whatever the path, the destination is only one, timeless, immovable... whichever street we walk on, we take one step, two steps, three steps forward, and we instantly go back in time one century, two centuries, three centuries; every nook and cranny we walk through has been or is an alibi of inspiration for poets, singers, musicians, artists who, from time immemorial up to modernity, spread in this city a perfume of culture, a unique odour that subsists in the ochre colour of the walls and the wrinkled granite parallelepipeds on the ground.

II

The shadow of the footsteps, at last, rests on the top, the wide square of the University; it is here, on the opposite side of the heart, somewhere, in a classroom, that they wait for the last student of the morning, whose name we have just heard, An-tó-nio!, the other students, already seated, are waiting for the last of them, António, to come in and sit down, so that the poetic art class can start; before burning the last cigarette between the yellow nicotine fingers, and before sitting down, the professor had already written on the blackboard on the wall: the cloak hanging, a beggar, the black wing on the side, the raven's soot that hangs the shadow from its beak, without ears or eyes, the day shelters it with its black cloak...

Avenida Sá da Bandeira – Coimbra

I

He sits, as he always does, in a corner at the back of the café *pigalle*, watching the waiter with the tray flying in space; some mineral water and an espresso!, that's what António said, in a low voice, and that's what he heard the waiter repeat, to someone behind the counter, in a clamour of rattling resonant voices; what he had asked flew in seconds from the counter in front of him, the white tiled table where he had already put the book (the book he read, and read, and read, the Miguel Torga book of his passion), also, the pencil and the notebook; he sipped to the last drop the water and the coffee, swallowing them in short sips; he remembered that he no longer knew anyone, since he had been there for the last time, while he was still a child; people had changed and with them the houses, the cafés, the places, what was the Café *Pigalle* is now a shopping centre, what was the Café Continental now is a ready-to-wear clothes shop; but the sloping street, falling on the road to the market, remains unchanged; he looked, however, with his memory, at the circle left by the bottom of the glass bottle on the table top, and remembered the tables and chairs made by hand by a carpenter in a carpentry shop, made with pieces of solid pine, then painted with a dark brown brush.

II

He also remembered the warmth of the old tree nooks and crannies, around here, in the garden opposite, the dozen exposed tables, leaning against the white walls, the hand painted tile waist at the middle of the white wall, the bottles in a row, full of dust, the shelves nailed to the bottom, on the wall of Café *Pigalle*; behind the counter, that piece of wood, of a tree, the little tradition that marked the distance between the warm memory of ancient times and the harsh cold of nowadays, the heat that the oxidised deny, the place of non-mirrors, of non-glare, of non-metal, of non-metal... of non-... of non-...

UNIVERSITY COURTYARD – COIMBRA

I

His memory suddenly jumped to the endless bookshelves. There are more than two hundred and fifty thousand ancient relics, preserved with the help of colonies of bats that live together in the Joanina Library and feed on insects during the night; the law of probabilities provides two hundred and fifty thousand books, which can be consulted by António and Aphrodite; we must now ask ourselves what strange and powerful force pushed the decision of both, to place themselves side by side and, each with their right hand on the same volume, the same book lined up on the bookcase, and at the same time touch it with their fingers stretched out, saying: you, you are the chosen one (not all of them will be, as we know), that volume bound of paper to book, and it was not because it had the importance that it had, a simple name engraved on the cover, the title of the book was a minor detail, at the time... we said that they both chose it, at the same time, they both tried to remove it from the bookcase, and in the hands of both the book would fall, tumbling back with its spine; we will ask ourselves about what made them look at each other and say: sorry! words said at exactly the same time, and both sighing, oh!; which, adding up, are two ohs, also said at the same time, in each other's echo; we wanted to find out what made them say, over and over again: you take it! you take it! you take it! no, you were here first! no, you were the one who arrived first... they interrupted one another in this game of deaf words, and decided to bring, both of them, the same volume to the table, they would consult it in collective group work, because of the circumstances, of the happy coincidence, we will say, because of chance.

II

My name is Aphrodite; mine, António; I study Romance Languages; I study Law; I live at Ferreira Borges; I, at Sub-Ripas Street... they exchanged telephone numbers, after taking some notes about the volume they had in front of them, after collecting some information on their notebooks, bio-bibliographical data, everything of minor importance, compared with the incident at the beginning, which we have already reported in detail; then, when saying goodbye: see you... see you...

III

António was walking along the sad street, the street with a bitter appearance, the street pregnant with words, the street bent by the weight of letters, sentences, books; he also carried the load of what he read in the eyes, in the face, in the gestures of... not in the volume, in the book, in the bookcase, in the space that shelters two hundred and fifty thousand names of books; he knows he is intoxicated, not with poets, not with triplets... *redondilha*[1]... sonnets...

IV

He put in ink and paper, he put in ink and paper, he put in numbers, he put Aphrodite's countenance in the void, until his eyes flickered, dazzled, like mosquitoes spinning around him, he tried to free himself of the rhyme, to remember Aphrodite's expression, her face, however, he remained embedded in a scattered countenance, in a confusion of art and poetic sounds; he walked in a silly manner and foolishly, when he got home, desperate; he slammed the door and locked it; inside, he reflected sitting at the kitchen table, he was confused, he lacked lucidity; only with weak illumination, he did not receive enough light to explain what had happened, he got up, maybe by opening the refrigerator some fresh air could come from inside to air his brain, to clarify ideas; nothing!

V

He stood up and, with the palm of his hand, stroked the hair from the forehead to the back of the neck, looking

---

1   TN – Redondilha is the verse of five or seven syllables.

at his reflection on the window panes; not a sign, a simple explanation for... he sat down and got up again, measured himself from his forehead all the way down, with his eyes focused on the tip of his feet, then he sat with the notebook in his hand, the pencil scribbling the paper, on the table, the arm with his elbow resting holding his head sideways, he wrote and scribbled the words he had collected in the library, the writing notes he had on the sheets of paper; the six numbers of the telephone were saved, in line, in a row; he tried to remember the face, the expression of the face, a trait of the image, Aphrodite's face, and nothing!; the hand only rested when the last stroke in the scribbled poem fell inside the dustbin; he also crushed, with the fingertips, the transparent surface of the glass, the drops of water running through the window, and, like a Braille reader, took them to the brain, stroking, once again, with the fingers as a comb, the hair from the forehead to the back of the neck...

República Square 1 – Coimbra

I

At ten o'clock in the morning, the bus was running up the street and Aphrodite was walking down the cobbled pavement, the cars were beeping in traffic, and the women were wrangling in the square; at five past ten in the morning, Aphrodite got on the bus, she punched her ticket with her left hand, and straightened her sunglasses above her fringe with her right hand; the driver – wearing a blue tie on the long, narrow white shirt – leaned back on his seat, raising his head, following Aphrodite with his eyes in the rear-view mirror, seeing her quickly swinging her body along the aisle, with her bag on her shoulder, her arms in the air, grabbing the stanchion... her body and hands were slim, sensual, grabbing the stanchion... he saw that she took her hand to her head, held the handle, releasing the band from her fragrant hair at the back, and, with the fervour of her lips dyed red, she replied good morning to her neighbour, Dona Rosa, who was sitting in the row with cushioned seats, at the back of the bus; she then remained silent, and the young woman, Aphrodite, with a black cape on her back, stood looking at the ground, thinking: poor Dona Rosa, almost ninety years old and so dedicated, carrying in her arms, throughout her body, first thing in the morning, bags filled with fruit, vegetables, offal, meat, fish; Aphrodite moved a little away from Dona Rosa, approaching the door to get out, and so as not to mix her perfumed scent with the smell of fish, entrenched in Dona Rosa's body and clothes; the bus went down the street and stopped; Aphrodite got off the bus and walked up the street in the opposite direction, further ahead she said hello to a friend who got off at the stop, and jumped on one foot to the other side of the road, she was in a hurry blocked by her tight skirt; she accompanied her hello! with a goodbye wave, her slender hand full of shiny rings on her long fingertips, she exhibited long painted nails, banging her metallic fist filled with bracelets; on the other side, her friend answered hello!, also with coloured nails and lips, equally plump, tanned down her shoulders, up to where the neckline died; the two friends seemed to look at each other in the reflection of the mirror, like twins; Aphrodite carried a dark light in her eyes, blue sea eyes, very blue... thick, hard eyelashes pointed upwards, towards the sky, blue...

II

The passers-by walked in the street, slowly strolling along the way, others were crumpled on the garden benches, and almost fell asleep, while others, attentive and wide awake, pinned their eyes on pedestrians, jumped from Aphrodite's legs to her lips, she who was walking along; then their eyes stuck to her hips and from there they went beyond the black skirt, tight, only stopping at the shrill sound of the whistle of a hasty driver, who, second in line, gestured inside his passenger compartment, pointing to the green light; Aphrodite remained undisturbed, in the same pace, on her way to the University, carrying under her left arm, firm and straight, a large briefcase with books; she was in a hurry, always walking, at the same time attentive to everything around her; it's not that she needed to relearn the way to the University, it's not that she needed to relearn the shortcuts of the streets in the city, since she had frequently walked by the garden benches, by República Square, near the pharmacy... but that morning, at half past ten, she was taken aback by an old man behind her asking: hey miss, please stop! tell me which button to press to get this thing off; said the old man with the trembling voice of his old age, a dirty, stinky old man, who interrupted Aphrodite, wrapped up in her own thoughts, an old man who was standing there by the condom machine, next to the central door of the pharmacy; Aphrodite, didn't answer him and continued walking, thinking out loud: was the old man messing with me? wow, an old man who can hardly stand up, an old man who drags his boots along the pavement, a man of advanced age and time, who has already reached the invalidity period, bent, trembling, why would he want a pack of condoms?, you've got to be kidding me!, she turned her back to him and walked on, disturbed... but she couldn't forget about him, all pensive, behind her...

III

As she walked, she thought: he approached me in the street to find out which button to press to get the condoms... on second thought, when she placed her hand on her conscience (or her conscience on her hand), saying to herself, in a burst of respect and tolerance towards others: poor old man, you shouldn't leave anyone without an answer, much less an old man... she tried (if there was still time) to recover from the wrongdoing, from the thoughtless behaviour she had engaged in, she looked back and shouted from afar: look, sir, press all the buttons, one of them will give you what you want!; having said that, she was serene with relief, still less heavy on her conscience, and walking happily, for she had performed the good deed of the day.

IV

Unexpectedly, in a split second, she turned and looked back... she opened her eyes, astonished!, she was overwhelmed, her shaking face reddened, her heart beating strongly, almost in a state of shock, when she saw at the end of the street, near the pharmacy, the pharmacist himself, in a white coat, who came out of the pharmacy and, in a sudden and sensible way, put his right hand on the shoulder of the old man and... Aphrodite saw the pharmacist accompanying the tender old man, she saw the pharmacist helping the happy old man, she observed, with her eyes wide open, the pharmacist simply helping the old man, and he, toothless, with that happy face that boys usually have on, he, nested under the arm of the pharmacist, both of them slowly crossing the street, side by side with each other... and finally she saw the pharmacist pointing with his hand in the other direction, pointing and telling him: it's there!, in that parking ticket machine, that you have to insert the coin to collect the ticket! the man in the white coat had explained to the old man all the details necessary to put the coin in the parking meter, which would then throw up a little paper to him... so: first he would have to stick the coin in the slot, then the machine would return a ticket that he would have to place inside the car... the small old car, as old as time itself, the car already immobilised in the background, in the República Square car park.

República Square 2 – Coimbra

I

Saturday, six o'clock in the morning, the sunrise by the stairs of the Academic Association: as if appearing from inside a dark tunnel of night, one, two, three, five, fifteen, twenty-two, thirty-six, forty-five black figures in a cloak and cassock, suitcases and luggage on their back; a coach shining and a driver - the one wearing a blue tie on the long, narrow white shirt – smashed a flannel cloth in his hand, polishing the shine of the metals; another driver, dressed in a similar way to the first one, folded into the luggage hold, lining up the double bass case alongside the cello case, the trombone with the five violin set, plus the clarinets, the oboe, and the orchestral flutes; hey!, said the first driver (sticking with his fingers the flannel on the door of the car's dashboard): bring the guitars, let's pack them in the back, next to the trolley suitcases; there was another black wooden box with bookshelves and score books, which was already on the side, on the other side of the coach…

II

The Portuguese guitars, with a differentiated privilege, joined the musicians seated in the coach seats, and played, tuned, to the sound of voices, the Ballad of Farewell of the Fifth Legal Year, an original song recently composed by Rui Lucas, António Vicente, and João Paulo Sousa.

III

Integrated in the Orchestra of the Academic Choir of Coimbra, in the year of his centenary, António (the poet and musician of words) went on tour; that time he was going to Paris, to the city of Lights, where the writer Eça de Queirós had worked as a consul a century ago…

GALA STREET – COIMBRA

I

Come in, my friend, good evening!; at the arrival of an old man, António uncrossed his legs, got up and rushed to get him a seat; oh, thank you!, good evening to all of you!, the old man said while coughing because of catarrh; then he hid behind the newspaper, going through the pages without reading them; finally, he folded it and left it on the nearest table; a few moments later he stretched himself on his side drawing tobacco from his trouser pocket, looked at the cigarettes in a row, chose one and lit its tip; when he inhaled a puff of smoke, the fire brightened his face; a cachaça, please, oh! and if anyone feels like having a drink, just ask for it!, oh, the old man vociferated, as usual whenever he came to that tavern; the bunch of laurel and the demijohn hung at the entrance, above the stonework, indicated the dark tavern's guardhouse.

II

In the tavern, people were attracted by the smell of fried small sardines and pickled sauce, the darkness and cool air of the basement on summer days, the dirt in the glasses that dictated the wine variety (the red from the closed up barrel); three or four tables around a dozen pine benches, and the wooden counter with the marble top, dappled with black stains, hiding the tavern's half behind it; the old man stretched out, crossed, and uncrossed his legs, asked for one more glass, amidst the silence of fear around him; there was a spectre on the faces of the others, those who were left in nooks and crannies at night; the weather was cold, and it was almost closing time; the old man, wearing a Basque beret over his eyes, his grey suit with black stripes, was drinking in short sips, seven already gone!... but around him there was nothing to count; the tavern keeper, with his apron, leaving the counter, curving at the tables, collecting the empty glasses, dragging the seats under the tables, while the old man hung his eyes on the display case of boiled eggs and liver cooked in onions, diverted to the counter; the other men around him admired his strength, they were afraid of him, and not only because of the dreadful figure with the wrinkled forehead, of the sideburns hanging through his thick beard, of his look of a beggar, dishevelled and grey; it was also because the old man, a confessed murderer, had served twenty-five years in prison, in what had been, until today, his second home... as usual, he would come there every night to soothe his spirit and get warm, to sleep among the cardboard boxes by the market; the tavern keeper would push everyone out as he swept the floor, towards the door, everything at the end of the night would be quiet in a silence like that of a tomb...

III

Only the singing of the birds would call the rain for the next day; and the old man, dragging his footsteps, wandered the street in search of a corner, which was not the singing of the birds...

IT WILL BE COLD IN THE AFTERNOON

TOWER OF THE UNIVERSITY 1 – COIMBRA

I

As soon as the doorbell rang, someone answered, I'm coming!, from inside, as usual, and in a few seconds the door opened with a dry sound; António climbed the stairs impatiently and felt, like a slap, the mixture of smells: mould, humidity, naphthalene; and he felt his stomach about to cause him to vomit, but persisted in familiarising himself with the scent of the house, stopping static, motionless, breathing lightly at the last flight of stairs; then he continued to climb up and turned left, greeted the old woman and her husband leaning against each other, drowsily, by the fireplace; he thought: its late into the night, and they are preparing to give the night a sleep, not the last one, just another sleep, around life; António walked in the opposite direction in the hallway, and now he could feel a pleasant smell, a familiar smell, an odour to which he had been getting used...

II

He announced himself and entered, locking the door from the inside; he approached Aphrodite from behind and kissed her fresh neck; that appealing body called him like a bright fruit on a tree branch; he surrounded her with his arms around her body, and then he kissed her on the back of the neck, and on the lips, pressed together, facing her; she avoided him with her hand on his mouth and begged him almost in a whisper: be not hasty! hush!; let's take it slowly... the old people have not yet gone to sleep! but he couldn't resist and nibbled one of her ears, then the other, he picked her up and knocked her over the bed; he began to unbutton her dress (he undid the buttons through the floppy holes, tiny fingers of other unnamed hands, open) and embraced her abdomen with his slender body; he raised her arms, taking off her blouse through her head; face down, with his hands on the bed, he trod his trousers on the ground; he threw himself on top of her again and kissed her on the shoulders and back, then on the lip of her ear, and he saw that she shivered in a tremor, as if she were suspended, voluble, trembling in his arms...

III

Outside, you could hear the gutter dripping on the roof, and moments later, the rain fell heavily on the tiles...

TOWER OF THE UNIVERSITY 2 – COIMBRA

I

A week later I visited Aphrodite; she was sitting at the kitchen table and had a glass and a jug of water in front of her; she filled the glass and took it to her mouth, sipped it, and sighed; attentive, I waited for her to speak, and I wasn't surprised that she called me on the phone, nervous, so urgently (maybe because I celebrated life after twenty-five years), and I wasn't too surprised that she told me to sit in front of her, at the kitchen table; I remained there for a few minutes in front of her; after looking me in the eye, Aphrodite said: prepare yourself... a brief silence, then she suspended the silence, she let out a long sigh; she stood up and walked in slow steps around the table, around me, circumspect and silent; she stopped, she looked at me, and then she took my arm, she placed herself facing me, her eyes narrowed on mine, I saw that she had difficulty getting rid of the words, then she dropped her heavy hands on my arms crossed over the table, saying: the tower of the University fell on me, with the bell of the chapel ringing, when I went to the doctor this morning, and he, with the lab tests from a month ago standing on the desk in his office, told me: the result was. ... positive! he said I was a carrier...

II

I got up from the seat as if I had been pushed by a spring and released a muffled cry with my hand in my mouth; it was as if I had been struck by an electric shock, or as if a helpless hill had fallen on my head, it was as if there was no more day, and a light had been extinguished over my eyes, it was as if a thunderbolt had struck me from top to bottom... while sobbing among words and crying, Aphrodite clamoured: I couldn't have warned you before, for I myself didn't know I was a carrier, I didn't know!; trusting in others, I became careless of myself, and you, trusting in me, became careless of yourself; António suspended his silence and, little by little, condemned: I who have read and written so much... and who had the dream of being a poet, a noble... like António, with his adjective surname[1]... and now, like him: a poet with Anto's illness... sick!, only a quarter of a century old...

---

1 TN – António Nobre's surname is the Portuguese word for "noble".

OLD SQUARE – COIMBRA

I

From up here, through Ferreira Borges' window[1], the view to the Old Square, what words might we use to describe the beauty of three doves flying diagonally, twirling in the air in a circle, once, twice, in a spiral, and finally landing in the middle of the Square?; as they fall on the stones of the ground, the doves, coming from the sky, we can imagine that, in a moment, others will follow (better still, they will imitate the flight), in this rain of doves that we are used to seeing in the Old Square.

II

Following the cogitation, we saw that a new stampede of doves fell from the air again over the Square, others followed it, and there are already so many, with their wings spread, twirling here and there, that we lost count; the tails of the doves, like the wings rolled up like a fan, their small and trembling paws walking on the ground in circles, cooing noisily, until Dona Angelina, after going down the stairs, appeared at the door of the house; she was carrying a plate on her left hand, and with her right hand, in gestures followed by the thousands of birds' eyes, with her fingers she plunged the grains on the plate and, throwing them into the air, they looked like raindrops lying on the stony ground, here and there, around and above the animals, in a whirlwind, uneasy; the woman turned left and the doves followed her footsteps, she turned right and the animals trailed her; we will never have the ability to scrutinise what is in the minds of animals that act in this way, following Dona Angelina to and fro, nor will we be able to make any judgements about their self-interested, selfish, greedy, calculating, vile behaviour... at best, we may be able to say that animals act in favour of the satisfaction of their instincts, for the benefit of their basic needs, in

---

1 TN – Ferreira Borges is the name of one of the streets bordering the Old Square in Coimbra.

short, and in a nutshell, they go round and round, pecking at the stoned ground, with the intention of satiating and gathering grains with which to satisfy their hunger.

III

A boy was walking nearby, with his father holding his hand, and when he saw the doves in the square, he threw himself, contrary to the wishes of his father, who still tried to stop him, and squatted next to the clouds of birds, which immediately began to peck at the rice cake that the innocent boy was holding in his hands, breaking it into crumbs in front of him; other clouds of birds fell from the roofs and flew diagonally down, then coiled up around the child, and the father waved his arms, shaking himself, his son and the doves, trying to free himself from that Hitchcockian bird film; but let it be stressed, and only then will it become more remarkable and real, what we were saying: that animals are opportunistic and take advantage of the most fragile ones; this is quite true, and it also happens to men... but for now let us leave ourselves in these ellipses, for they are creative in our minds, and will probably find an end to this apparently banal episode, in which there are doves and fathers, by the hands of children, in an old square.

Quinta das Lágrimas – Coimbra

I

Tears are river, river is water, water is light, light is writing, writing is words, words are tears, tears are music (when they fall into the river); tears are river...

II

He read the poem to Aphrodite, who lay on the garden bench, her head resting on António's thigh, who was stroking her hair; he also read to her the tale of Pedro and Inês, the story of a secret love, in which tears are a river, a river is water, water is light, light is writing, writing is words, words are tears, tears are... tears are eternal... Aphrodite interrupted, and António continued: tears can go from one end of the world to the other, they can go from one time to another, like those of Pedro and Inês, who were sent to us by history, from the past, through a tunnel, stuck inside a little wooden boat, written with the feather on paper, written with promises of eternal love... these words followed, hidden, no more than five hundred metres away, from the Quinta, where Pedro was, to the Palace of the convent of Santa Clara-a-Velha, where Inês was; it is certain that, from the outside world to the inside world, from the Quinta, where Pedro lived, to the Palace of the Convent, where Inês lived, the little wooden boat took love from one corner to the other, through the river of tears, the love that affirmed itself as unique, infinite, everlasting... said António to Aphrodite, and she nodded, looking up to him...

III

In the circle of darkness that completes the day, with my hands up and the pen pointed at my back, I stood still, holding one of the notebooks, and began the work of writing: then, I say rose, I say homeland, I say peace; inside, a flame burns, devouring me, a blade that bites me, sets me on fire, and destroys me; faded, the sap-ink falls unscathed on the paper, like petals of melancholy in the gestures and hot forged fire in the fingers, I palpate a ripe apple on your bosom; transfigured into António, no, into a poet, I dye the paper with ink, I'm sorry!, that was a warm voice in me, the other in me, who, for a moment, revealed himself...

SUB-RIPAS STREET – COIMBRA

I

I had the narrow bed under the staircase, which gave me the privilege of being able to count the steps of the guests, of knowing what time people arrived, if people went out, if people came in, I could make a complete inventory of the feet that rustled on the carpet of the staircase, on their tiptoes, almost in silence, sometimes, often, not wanting to announce themselves; the bed in the staircase was the only sacrarium of secrets in the house; I could, if I wanted, conduct business in the sale of secrets; and so I had on the bedside table, beside me, my notebook, my watch, my pencil and my flute; but on grey winter afternoons, when I arrived to the pensive room, feverish, full of words like a pinecone, pregnant with that poison which are the letters together in syllables, words with meaning, knowing that a story should begin at one end, somewhere, and that the distance between the first and the last word is where the poem stands, the tale, the novel, written line by line... six hundred lines, written for nothing – knowing also that, with words, we can reach perfection, beauty, and with them, words, one cannot be too careful; I pulled out the notebook and the pencil, and, lying down on my stomach, I began to write: we only truly die when our place at the table is taken, then we really cease to exist.

II

And I continued: my father died, and for a long time no one occupied that place, the place that was his, we were used to seeing him at the top of the table, sitting...So he died and remained there, or it was our memory of him, there, in that place, existing permanently, in invisible contours, a non-matter body, not alive; then it was the youngest, the children, who climbed up the empty armchair, with one knee, first, pushing with their hands, afterwards, with their short legs that did not reach the ground, with them hanging in the air, they felt like kings for a day when they occupied the top of the table; later, it was the visits, the friends who sat there, outlandishly unaware of the sacred history of that place; and only when the memory of a father who died is already very tenuous, the memory, which fades away until we hardly remember that he existed, do we begin to seize his place at the table, to occupy that place properly, the empty space which is nobody's land, as they say: right here, right now, there is nothing, really nothing!, and now he, my father, is definitely dead!

BAIXINHA – COIMBRA

I

With my nose smashed against the clothes shop window, I meditated on why I hadn't dared to go in, to learn about the spring-summer fashion trends; I had just arrived downtown and refused to try on the dresses that were on offer from the door to the street, I was afraid that I would wear them and look more beautiful, I was afraid of all that gracefulness, offered like that, and afraid of getting used to beauty, and then, when the time had passed and I got older, all wrinkled and sick, I was afraid I wouldn't be able to deal with the non-beauty of my skin, the non-beauty of my breasts, the non-beauty of my body; in short, I repeat: the non-beauty of my breasts and the non-beauty of my body... I remember, by the way, that I do not recall the mastery of the colour of his eyes, nor do I discern that which is the timbre of his voice; I know him as a musician of words, I do not know his musical preferences: I only know a few books that dominate his reading during day and night, the poems that can hurt him; I know a few words that can enter him and make him cry, I know a few books that can lead him to tears: the first of them, Nobre, also, Herberto, Calvin, Cella, Nemésio, Torga, Saramago, Eugénio, Sophia, Redol, Júdice, Borges, Agustina, Aquilino...

II

I know little about you!, even though you were inside me one random night, even though you tasted my skin, licking my infinite body; I wanted to trap you in the web of words, when you whisper in my ear, and mix them in a set of letters dyed of sound that drive me crazy; the writing undresses people, puts them naked in front of us, but I can't see you naked when I read you; I wanted to see my long fingers running through your skin, my wet lips running through your body, not so much to kiss you, but to distinguish your flavour, to know you inside your clothes, looking for you under the sheets, running through your pores millimetre by millimetre, cell by cell your flesh, to know and drink your poetry, to get drunk on it, and, hallucinating, to get naked and dance before you... then tell you that there is a dewy, red, flower, a rose inside me waiting for you to come, waiting for you to enter quickly into that night, that you seek with your teeth to bite my ear, my lips and my breasts, that you come and eat the aphrodisiac dinner of me; I will open myself like a sea shell and close you inside me, two molluscs inside one, merging, each one in the self of the other; I will wash you in the shower of my hair stretched backwards, to the back of my neck, and I will tell you about the taste of the water that overflows from this river; now tell me about the pleasure of that dagger crossed in me; tell me everything, much more than what the words want to tell me, when you write, and write to me, they which seem so simple... like the word caress... which goes far beyond the six letters with which you write it... I live in the eagerness to find a word, the last one, which will save us, an expression of mercy, the only one, which will bring you back to me... I believe that all that God has created, it was through the word.

Porta-Férrea – Coimbra

I

I said to Aphrodite: the poor man's buttered bread always falls on its face, and it had to happen, to me of all people: I took a kick in the shin on my left leg as I walked the Porta-Férrea; I bit my tongue so as not to scream, I contained the pain of anger on my red face, and the troupe, not happy with that, smacked me on the back as I ran away; they made fun of the poet-like student, short, angular boy-faced, book writer who dresses eccentrically, bizarrely, and who carried Stendhal under his arm; I sat down with Aphrodite on the garden bench, we talked, and I washed my soul, outside and inside, as I spoke...

II

At a certain point, I got to know him better, after we spent entire afternoons talking: he was not an only child, he had six siblings, he confessed to me; sometimes we spoke and listened more to each other's silences and sighs; short sentences, an occasional yes, a negative nod; I could feel the noise of his body stirring, sitting at the table, writing, with his elbows placed as a V, his arms raised under his chin, resting on the table top, two arms, two Vs, double V, double-u; the notebook and the pencil on the table top, he would say to me: listen to this poem, this prayer, and he would read aloud: Lord!, make me find poetry in the silence of the rainy mornings, in the calm of the stormy afternoons; Lord!, make me find poetry on the steep mountain path, on dark nights of astonishment; Lord!, make me find poetry on the echo of the walls of time, on the small particle of the atom; Lord!, make me find poetry in the transparency of the tear, in the light blue of the sea; Lord!, make me find poetry everlastingly, and allow me to bathe in it in a state of delirium, until the soul cries out, until the blood bursts forth and descends through tributaries, into the deepest labyrinth...

III

Unbelieving, António kneaded the poem-prayer dyed on the paper and threw it to the rubbish, uttering, as if spitting: so ignorant, so banal!

IV

It is beautiful to have an available line of silence, between your telephone and mine, through which words flow, words that are exchanged, that cross, that sometimes clash... yes, it is beautiful!, and have you thought about the infinity of words that we can exchange through that line of silence?; I hadn't thought of that!; and listen: a word can mean many others, it can go beyond the five, six or seven letters that it has, and it can have only five letters, as the word alone[1], and signify a book with two hundred written pages; yet there are words that are empty, and they don't go beyond the letters, together, which say... the word is a powerful weapon that writers always have at hand; armed with words and dreams, the one who writes is never alone and can overthrow the world; sometimes one word, one sentence brings down the Government of a Nation; a bag of newspapers full of words, which the newspaper vendor distributes in the morning, is more powerful than a lorry loaded with ammunition for the army with soldiers in line.

V

Anto!, whenever I read you, I find my life merging into yours, I hardly know where I end and where you begin; my eyes even hurt from reading you; I feel that my being has penetrated into you, into you, I no longer know where I end and where you begin...

---

1 TN – "Alone" is the English equivalent to the Portuguese word "Só". That two-letter word is the title of António Nobre's masterpiece.

VI

Anto of me: your regret, for my regret, you join;
your sorrow, for my sorrow, twins; your pain, for my pain...

SANTA CLARA – COIMBRA

I

The abbot and the gravedigger made a pact with death, for they, men, were also possessed by the flesh... in fact, there is still a bit of hanging land waiting for man's burial, so, as a cruel executioner, time, plus diseases, plus life's plans, in which people kill each other like beasts, animals... finally, they dictate this end of life, which is death; the abbot celebrates masses and entrusts his soul to God, the gravedigger in turn prays to him and entrusts his body to the earth; between them, says the abbot, what is the best entrustment?, the one that goes straight to the space of heaven?, or the one that follows the opposite path, thrusting itself into the earth, the hot hell, right in the centre of the Earth? the nuns move silently around their chores in the convent – they do not look at each other, they do not speak, they do not answer –, they get up and lie down praying, they carry the cilices clinging to the body and between their legs; they also do not know whether the echo of their sigh reaches the ears of God, or whether the sacrifices help to absolve them from their sins, from the nights with the abbot who sleeps with them... for twenty-five years of his life, not twenty-five days, not twenty-five hours; the proof of this truth is in those who were found in the rubble, and it is also written that the abbot lived within the monastery in sin of flesh with the novices, nuns and mothers, each and every one, sin of flesh with a man of cassock (the black cloak); and it was... twenty-five years?... or a few hours, minutes only, a second, a small instant like a bullet shot, which led him to death...

1889

CARQUEJA ALLEY – COIMBRA

I

I hear whispers and screams of girls together; I hear machines shaking in the sewing pedal; I hear children crying and noises of pots coming out of the windows; I can hear the boys' hoop spinning and jumping on the cobblestone in the street; I can hear voices of country girls on the banks of the Mondego, in the background, with rolled up bedsheets, lifting them up in the air and throwing them stridently on the wooden planks in front of them; there is a pure, simple, grounded world out there, and loutish people, bound by ropes of futility, people who will never understand the message of poets...

II

Once, like today, Augusto, I want to tell you about this decadent Coimbra, how much I am disgusted by the vanity of the students; the Faculty - and that of Law takes first place in line – remains in the darkness of the Middle Ages, courses that are of no use, black cloaks coming from shadows of ignorance and noisy wandering, which is what is more frequent!; vanity for what?, there is no job for so many people out there wandering the streets drunk, ignoramuses looking for what?, honour?, glory?

III

These people will never ever understand – I tell them from the Road of Beira – what *Purinha*[1] meant to me, and the light that illuminates what remains of her, the field, the spirit, the dream; these people will never understand what it means to truly love... what is love?; love is when one part of us ceases to exist and we are the tenderness extending into the other... that is love, love means the extension of the I into the beloved thing, as the poet said...

---

1 TN – Purinha means, in Portuguese, Little Pure One (feminine). This was the nickname that António Nobre gave to Margarida de Lucena, his girlfriend between 1890 and 1896. Her mother had requested her never to get married, so Purinha was unattainable, almost unreal.

IV

I picked up the steaming cup of tea beside me, and, sitting with the pen and paper on the table top, I continue to write: I want to depict the failure of the times in this city, for there are days when I strain every nerve around a text for the newspaper, a poem for a magazine, and what do I find?: streetwalkers, the unhealthy bohemian life, drunkenness, the softened taste of a crust of bread, flashy on the outside, entrenched and mouldy in its core, inside... I write you this letter to tell you that a wind of disease is blowing on my face and body, and I cannot hide the orbits of the eyes under the eyelashes to fall asleep, I cannot retain the image of the mask, and so I'm leaving this city where success has not managed to manifest in my spirit; I will not be missed, I will be no more than the fly's excrement in the shop window, or a shadow of a body for the burial of the martyrs; if I arrived here on my own, one day I shall leave this place to turn on all the shadow lights that burn within me and that will kill me; as for the impregnated air that clogs my lungs and the rubbish that swells my stomach, I want to throw them out and forget them; thank you; your brother, Anto.

Lixa – Felgueiras

I

Today, Saturday, I overslept and dreamed that I crouched in a garden looking for you, margarida[1], among other flowers; I was walking with my hands in the air, my eyes blindfolded by a dark handkerchief, looking for you, margarida, among other flowers... lucid lily[2]... Margarida Lucena... I dreamed of you and also of the sun on the beach of Figueira da Foz, the waves galloping on the sand, coming to nestle next to my book, the poem notebook... the notebook with poems that, in a heroic gesture, I saved, like Camões, from the waves of the sea... *skinny, like a poplar to which the vine ties itself, and her hair in bunches, bunches of grapes [...] her breasts might be like two nests [...] her mouth a pomegranate...* I still remember that Margarida stood there, her right hand leaning on her waist and her left holding the zinc bucket filled with water, the same water she poured out later in the middle of the courtyard, and on the flowers, like thirsty turtledoves singing to my grandmother who left home, for she wanted to see my bride with a veil of light, made of moonlight, falling on her back...

II

Dressed in almost black grey, the lark chirps sweet music from its beak, gorges and sings; as if the earth were burning hot, the lark hops and pecks at the grain; it rolls its eyelids in the globe of its eyes; the lark launches a shallow flight, shouting to the nest, raising its baton: and an orchestra of beaks in the air, out of tune, responds, with no other art than that of eating.

---

1 TN – The Portuguese word "margarida" means "daisy". Like in English, it can be the designation of a flower and the name of a woman.

2 TN – In Portuguese, there is a play of words with "lucid lily" (in Portuguese: "lúcida açucena") and "Margarida Lucena", which was the name of António Nobre's girlfriend.

III

The house of Seixo would be crowded on Sundays while the yellowish sun appeared behind the trees; the sun that would then spread into the courtyard and turn pink; the sun that would afterwards gain a pale colour, especially when it rose and spread through the roof of the house; the sun that in the evening became mixed with the smoke from the chimney, turned grey and disappeared, incorporated into the night.

RUE RACINE – PARIS

I

Such a bizarre costume: over the thick fisherman jumper, I have a knot in my throat when I jump over the edge of *Britania*; because I had not bidden farewell to Alberto, my great friend, the memories of Coimbra and *Purinha*; I had not bidden farewell to the sea of Leça and to the tanned Gabriel, and to the *whaler* Sun, with which one could cross the Atlantic; only Junqueiro joins me under my arm, like Fialho and others in the luggage.

II

For an embrace remains unsaid, the gesture of misfortune of a country marinating, when death accompanies my black clothes, and the light darkens the sound of my steps, agile and frail in the cobblestone, creaking; I am no longer the misfortune that assists me, nor the sorrow that hinders me; the cough blocks the smoke that comes out of my mouth, in puffs; I am a spectre of sputum...

III

It was Sunday, the twenty-sixth of October, five thirty-six in the morning, when I arrived in Paris; it was a dewy morning, the sky dressed in lead, and I was walking along the Saint-Germain boulevard up to number two at rue Racine; when I got home, I untied my cufflinks and the oxidised pin that secured the dark tie; I threw the white coat on the backrest of the chair, the white coat that was tightening the narrowness of the abdomen on a gold coin-button; I hid the eyepiece in my pocket and pushed the cane away from the front of my steps, putting it in a corner; as I walked to bed, I turned off all the lights behind me.

IV

The night disappeared in the cold of the morning and the day cleared up into a sleep; I could see from the window a city of lights, with the Seine running in the background, serene, with its water limited to the banks; I wrote words in silence, among the rumours of people walking in the streets and crossing over bridges...

V

Already sitting in the armchair, at home, wearing a robe, with my pipe in my left hand, my cognac in my right one, I resumed my readings with Baudelaire, Camilo and Balzac; with Herculano, João de Deus and Dante; with Antero, Flaubert and Camões; with Bernardim, Cervantes and Garrett; I live in a craving for writing, I learned more about political science, but still I do not reinforce the incessant search for poetry, inside and outside the libraries of Paris...

VI

From Coimbra, with a pure heart, I write and remember: the pillages with friends in the henhouses of Conchada, the visits to Tentúgal in search of nuns and conventual flavours, the stay in Lousã, near a majestic castle, and, back in Coimbra, in the bosom of lamentations, blending in with the smell of taverns with marinated liver cooled off in the shop windows, tasting the Gândara wine, dirty, reddish, darkened at the bottom of the glasses; in Coimbra, I wear the impure and sweet memory of Ophelia, an aphrodisiac, who killed the soul of the poet, the poet who seeks patches for his illness, the disease of poetry that rots on the outside but gnaws on the inside...

VII

Verses are prayers...

RUE DES ÉCOLES – PARIS

I

He paid for the freight, came down from the caleche and walked for a hundred and fifty metres on a wide avenue; he asked a man in black, through gestures, what direction to take; he continued the walk, turned on to a street on the right, on to another to the left, again on the right, walked for about twenty metres and reached the rue des Écoles, a long road with tall buildings on either side; on the left, an old building, inside a stone wall; dragged to his weight, he crossed the iron gate, flanked by two columns at the entrance, and, already inside, he raised his eyes, gazing at large windows and balconies with balusters in white stone, and, in front of his contemplative face, a staircase, which he climbed, and entered through a dark wooden door, over two metres high, and, already inside, he made himself known to the gate-keeper, who installed him in a room, comfortably, in the middle of a wide hallway; under a fan he waited for a long time, sitting; the bright sun entered through the glass windows and hit the waxed wooden floor; he arranged numerous papers which he carried under his arm, then laid them on his knees and finally lined them up on the cushioned armchair, a twin to the one next to him; he almost fell asleep, all relaxed, when the gate-keeper appeared in front of him, saying: His Excellency the Consul is expecting you on the second floor, on the first door on the right!

II

That day I had a memorable talk with Eça about the white houses of the Mondego, built above the hill that goes down to the river, and the narrow stone paths, where the students, loutish, carousing freshmen, walk around trapped like animals on ropes in the middle of the troupes!, to which Eça, stroking his moustache and sticking his monocle on his eye, somewhat doubtful, exclaimed: I cannot believe it!; I insisted, adding: for what it is worth, the air in the street and in the attics is impregnated with a crazy, medieval bohemian life, the air one breathes is one of fear and boredom, if you don't believe it, my dear Eça, I fear for the return to the old Portugal, which is looking for the memory of itself, where nothing can be done to change it! then the great novelist concluded in the following terms: at least, may we know how to imitate, and may we observe Europe, this Paris on the banks of the Seine, far from the shabbiness of young people on their knees on the cobblestones, puking excesses from wine, from moonless nights, without hope for the future; finally, I reiterated: what they lack is food in their soul, the people of today, almost uncultured, not knowing what awaits them, are shaken like noisy flies, drunken fools, stuck in window curtains, in closed rooms at the end of summer...

III

The other day, in the five-storey house, right in the centre of Paris, while I sipped my *café au lait*, I listened to the roar of the Saint-Étienne du Mont bell, and wrote to Papa, letters and postcards, and to Alberto, one, two, three letters a day, Alberto about whom I also write in the Diary, the same Diary that he writes for me, words returned in blue ink; today I mentioned the inventory of martyrdom I go through, of the horrible suffering I am condemned to, comparable only to the *kicks in the shins* I got in Coimbra, in the years of degradation I spent there, which left bruises, sore injuries in my flesh, in my soft heart, the pain visible in my dark sunken eyes...

IV

Sampaio Bruno visited me one day in the dim street of Trévise; alas! I was deeply struck by that visit, because a wise man had entered my house, a man exiled in Paris for years, however, I still do not know what made Bruno leave his apartment, on the other side of the Seine, to commune with me on a day of such painful solitude?

Rue de La Valette – Paris

I

On a decadent Sunday, far away, in Paris, thousands of kilometres away, that is when the nostalgia hurts, and it hurts as much, or more, than a knife cut... I dreamt that I was receiving a black-edged letter from Georges and, surprised, I looked at it on both sides; I opened the envelope with the stylus and peered inside; I saw a piece of paper with sketches, amendments, scratches of letters and words from sad people; with astonishment in my eyes, I leafed through and read the letter, I reread it... amazed because, through it, I heard the weeping of voices of the people, I felt in the written words the consternation of the people, I was invaded by a chill because of the cry of the voices sobbing with sorrow, I could hear them together like hisses of wind in the streets, like the exasperated cries of brothers in affliction... I pulled out the pen, the nib, and wrote back; it was a poem of hope, which I sent without corrections, and what else could I do for Georges?

II

I threw the afternoon away through the sash window, and remained alone; I kept words on paper, converted letters into syllables; from the flame of oil came light, the moon became moonlight, while the letters created, from the gesture of the hand on the pen, with the nib turning, the hand unveiling the sounds that words contain, unveiling the language contrary to the silence that springs from the verses, from the darkness that falls from amazement and suspends images of spikes bursting from the earth; while the river lies in the waves, the insomnia of the fish persists, the tears are born from the fountains, and tenderness falls from the eyes.

III

Dona Carlota looked at me from top to bottom and said: I think you look paler this morning, do you have consumption in your soul?, in fact, I don't know what I feel, I answered, but the two daughters of the housekeeper, coming from school, used to come to see me and I gave them alms [...] now, as soon as they see me, they all tremble, poor things, I call them by the window and they run away scared...

IV

Dona Carlota, a short woman, approached me with her dress covered with little dots, her round freckled face... she was a mountain of sweetness: broad-shouldered, plump body and thighs; she regretted the frame of the narrow doors, which always bumped into her; at times she used to bring me smoking hot linden tea and two lighted candles on a tray, inflamed; she promised the Lady a novena and began to sing, moaning for Dona Júlia... I remember two foxes in the Law exam, in the first and second years, years lost and only found later in the poetry of Boémia Nova[1] and in the scattered newspapers!, I remember the boxing scene in the middle of the Larga street... after the passionate debates about literature, a plethora, from where I came out vexed, with my heart groaning with humiliation; when they saw me sad, the big-mouthed people gossiped, there's a passion of Coimbra there!, and indeed there was, and there was heat and there was fever, it was the passion of poetry.

V

Lying in the alcove brooding, with the moonlight coming in through the window, he wept for the undertaker who made a pact with death; tidying up his bundle of clothes, with a bunch of books and notebooks (he never forgot about his poems), he walked among the lights of Paris; Anto was celebrating his twenty-fifth birthday and he wants to offer himself a gift; there isn't much money, though, that's why he takes ALONE to Léon Vanier, the

---

1 TN – Boémia Nova was the name of a magazine launched in Coimbra, in 1889, directed by António Nobre, among others. The magazine intended to combat the intellectual decadence of Coimbra, the absence of a channel through which young writers could show their work.

maternity hospital which is going to help him with the child birth of his notebook, with more than two hundred typed pages...

VI

More than the evil, the evil of Anto, unstoppable, I have made myself dispossessed of me, a dandy who is lethargic towards me, in a pain that does not stop; I look around and what do I see: the boredom, the sleep of death seizing the soul, the sad fate that they beseeched in Coimbra, this restlessness that does not leave me, the funereal macabre that seizes my bones; at least while I live, you can count on Anto, who is yours, and take from him, from him alone, in a repeated edition of the other self, the noble Anthony... from the bookshop Aillaud, I have earned a thousand francs, for the second edition of ALONE.

VII

I write a postcard to Alberto while I inhale some smoke from the new wooden pipe I ordered from Coimbra; before inspiration hinders me, I will also write to Papa about Anto's debts, which increase week by week: I bought a new velvet suit, took photographs, paid for medicines at the pharmacy, stamps at the post office, a pair of socks, a pair of gloves, a tie, a necklace, an umbrella, a felt hat, a shirt, a jar of salts, a perfume, the newspapers of the week, books... oh!, the books, the greatest temptation, the list of books: Fialho, Eça, Cervantes, Bocage, Bernardim, Prévost, Corneille, Lesage, Racine... besides the Bible, Shakespeare and Verlaine; I want to buy a bicycle, and the souvenirs for Margarida, Alberto, Augusto... the debts add up to a thousand, three hundred and seventy-five francs.

VIII

I was hit by a car at the Boul'Mich, and could have died; with frightened people turning their heads, and I, in the middle of the stretch of road, when I saw the car approaching, coming at full speed, deranged, I began to run, in an attempt to jump onto the pavement on the other side of the street; however, it was too late and I was violently hit by the front, which suddenly appeared in the background, leaving a deathly silence in the rear, an oh!, the roar by the crowd walking by; the people walking up and down the pavement looked at me again, and, in amazement, they saw that I had been caught on the side, and despite the troubled heart, in a restless beat, I was alive after all, and that was good; with the darkness of the night moving over the houses and streets, lights were already abounding in the lamps that doubled in mirrors of the water puddle scattered on the ground.

IX

Only what belongs to you is yours!; with my arm tied to my chest, limited in my gestures, he moved the shadow of his body along the streets, pulling the smoke from each verse; with a groaning heart, he remembered dead ancestors, for it is of them that one is born, it is for them that one lives, and it is for them that one runs, in haste, like all those who suffer...

X

Paris, Bordeaux, Irún, Pampilhosa, stuck in a third class train, with his diploma under his debilitated arm... he sighs and speaks to himself, António, looking down from his stature: this is the degree that leads me to the Consulate, through Eça, recommended by Eça.

XI

But his poor health prevented him from pursuing the dream; it was as if a bird hit the transparency of glass, and fell to his feet, almost entirely plucked, exsanguinated, dying; a breath of life fallen on the pavement, only a drop of water into its beak might save him; he then raised its head to life, as if he could still turn on the light switch tenuously: he went to the door of Seixo, Monte Estoril, and, tearing the Atlantic apart, searched for comfort for the malaise in New York, Washington, Baltimore, but *Never-more...*

CASCAIS – PENAFIEL

I

Teach me what you know, sisters, for all I want is to learn: the toils of agriculture, the corn harvest, the cultivation of the land, the vine propping; I will be a man all made of ears to listen to you... help me!...

II

This pain in my chest that breaks me, this anxious breathing to which I am committed, this black cushion on which I lie, this sad morbidity in which I remain, this dim light in which I look at myself, this firm sorrow that is never released, this hard land that imprisons me, this green vine in which I touch myself; this serene look in which I remain.

III

I will not be light, tether, anchor, fetus, just...

IV

Will you remember me, in the afternoon, when I leave you poems at your door?, it's just that...

V

(A cough out of the deep, from the inside, cut the sentence in half, like a sheet of paper that is torn!)

VI

Will you remember me, in the afternoon?, and will you take care...

VII

(Again the cough, repeated with effort, clattering); the hand flattened over the mouth, the body bowing towards the ground; the legs oscillating while walking, arms twisted in the air; eyes closed, as if for a moment the light of the world also darkened the soul...

IT WILL BE COLD IN THE AFTERNOON

FUNCHAL – MADEIRA

I

She is accompanied by a sad Newfoundland dog, which will soon take her to the cold grave once and for all [...] and when I hear her dry and thin cough, I think I hear in a workshop the plates of her coffin preaching!, the sad fate of poor consumptive, a fate just like mine, which made me become sick and weep, fulfilling the prophecy of Dona Carlota: oh, what a poor child! Our Lady made him so unhappy... I climbed the island, eager to breathe good miraculous air, not so much because of the consumption which made me stunted, but rather because of the cure for this evil; I was gasping and a rumbling emerged in my chest like a roar interspersed with cavernous cough; twin frogs in the lakes, croaking to the warm, dark and damp, rainy and sad night, falling from the sky onto the flowers; an old woman came to the window, with the watering can inclined, and watered the rain-soaked flowers, twice dewy, the flowers, beautiful, twice, the flowers...

II

Suffering António's woes, Anto is seen searching; slim, a walking skeleton, in dribs and drabs, lost in the autumn's cold, still so spring, and already autumn!, *my cup of milk!, and it was on the thirteenth...* he cried the cold fever, the tremor of pain in his body, a pain greater than longing!, a peasant woman passing by, barefoot and with a bag of wet linseed on her back, stretched out her right hand, pointing: up there at the top, the sun burns the evil beast!, Koch's bacillus!

III

Oh!, tragedy, my fate, sing my verses in the light of a paraffin lamp, put on the white garment and go down the road to announce to the poor that I exist and I die for you, my faithful friend, my beloved blood brother, ardent friendship of heart, Oliveira[1] of olive, of capital letter A for *azeite*[2], of a tree that leads me to the grave, to the ditch, in the company of a dog, the only one who watches over me until the *Tapada das Setes Cruzes...*

IV

City of Funchal: Alberto, as you know, I have a visceral love for Oliveira, because each verse I write is an Olive branch; you know that the fruit is as necessary to the poem as the rosemary branch to the passion of Christ, in the olive garden, before Easter; you know the framing of the window in the balcony, the trunk of the olive tree crowded with lichens, and the branch of the green that carves the transparent glass; you know about the magnifying glass that increases the size of the black fruit; you know about the oily juice, pure olive oil, light and food of souls in the tomb, in the church, in the chapel; you know about the golden and bright trickle that quenches the palate of thirsting mouths, like the dry shell on the sand of the beach; you know about the olive tree, the surname of ancestors, of people who immortalised the gesture of the wind, in the movement of living branches, down to the ground; you know about the stream of complicity, of speech, and of touch. Yours, Anto.

V

We came all this way, all in our Carnival costumes, and we want to see the poet, in the flesh!, the girls said well, to which the chamberlain replied: the poet is unwell, come back tomorrow, perhaps, in the meantime, he will get better.

VI

---

1   TN – In Portuguese, Oliveira is a surname. Its meaning is "olive tree". It might be important to underline that one of António Nobre's closest friends was Alberto d'Oliveira (1873 – 1940), a poet who also attended the university in Coimbra and who founded the magazine Boémia Nova with Nobre.

2   TN – "Azeite" is the Portuguese word for olive oil.

Well, the next day the poet waited and waited, one hour, two, three hours in the hotel lobby, and the girls without masks did not return; still, he dedicated a poem to the girls, the daughters of the Countess, before moving on to Seixo.

VII

A poet alone, in a solitary house; he who departed from here, one day, is not the same who returns now!, said a servant from the house of Seixo; to this poor sage, the illness stole the flesh out of the bones, the features off his face, and the light from his eyes!, said another servant from the house of Seixo; the other day, on a steamer, in farewell, wrapping his arms around Augusto, Anto was going somewhere where there was no hope of coming back... he was wearing the long monk sackcloth, which fell from his back like from an emeritus bishop, he was trembling as he walked...

CLARAVEL – DAVOS

I

I spent three days at Davos-Platz, where I languished, and jumped into the snows of Claravel, a village with four remote houses by the mountains, resting for ten hours on a chair, without a soul and with the consumption declared; Margarida, the one who had grown up in the garden of the Estrada da Beira, had withered like me, now; I visited the city of Geneva, I settled in Lausanne, by the Leman, I was also in Germany, and I travelled to the Netherlands, Belgium... oh, travelling is an illusion, the whole planet is zero.

II

I have not yet spoken of the temple of the Aemenium[1], nor of the ruins of Conímbriga, I have not told the story of the conqueror, Afonso Henriques, nor of the exploits of D. Sancho I, the populating king, and his son... although I walked through the streets of Coimbra, and entered and left the church of Santa Cruz, with my feet above and my mind under the stones where they are now buried; I did not invoke Luís de Camões, nor Leanor, unsecured; I only spoke of the House of the Palace of Sub-Ripas, of the Tower of Anto and of António who became Anto, a metamorphosis of himself; and the country girls leaning over the river, the affable Purinha, who in her bosom caresses me; I spoke of men who climb the Mondego by canoe, wielding the stick, stuck to the bottom of the waters.

III

Nothing was said about the churchyard of Santa Cruz, where the bride used to sleep on sleepless nights, and the Mermaid's Garden, an idyllic lost paradise, the top of a city that was made from thinking and to think, a city to meditate and to meditate on; António, an avatar of himself,

---

1 TN – Aeminium is the ancient name of the city of Coimbra.

waits for the night to light the darkness, waits for the time of the trumpets in the street; *rumour has it that it was the passion* that made him fall ill, walking to the grave, to a *hotel of bones,* walking by his foot among the trees, with his fate in his hand... so early, so young; on a dewy night, when the village bells tolled, plangent...

IT WILL BE COLD IN THE AFTERNOON

CASCAIS E MONTE ESTORIL – LISBOA

I

António goes from calvary to calvary, invoking nature to remove the trees' skeletons from the bottom of the wells; he also invokes Ophelia, the pale and blond woman, a vision of the fateful love that he poured on the stones this autumn and that exhumes him to death; Anto, the cloud walker who bleeds, asking the eagles to come and eat his corpse in the midst of the lands; *Anrique, from Portugal of the ninth century*, comes to take the glimmer of light from the fainting lamp, 'cause it's midnight already!, and the worms are at the door wanting to come in; go and open the door for them and wait a minute with them in the living room, I'll be right down, said António, adding: I just want to take a rest after this Atlantic journey, stuck in the stuffy bunk of a boat, like in a child's cot; you see, the ocean has wrinkles and the back of the boat cannot stop softly stroking them when it goes by...

II

Anto, a poet facing the tomb, on the threshold of the grave, where I will finally find peace, the end of the atrocious suffering that takes me and with me the memory of this country facing the collapse, a *Portugal that only God can save*, the amorphous multitude, a package with a forthcoming expiry date... I will then be appeased, deep down, feeling good about myself and those who remain here, humble ones of the people, witnessing the memory of the days, amorphous, all of them...

CARREIROS – FOZ DO DOURO

I

Those words roaring in my ear: António, it will be cold this afternoon... it will be cold this afternoon... it will be cold this afternoon... down below the ground!, put on some warm clothes!, said my brother Augusto, entwining his arm over my back.

II

It was mid-March, the sixteenth, the last year of the nineteenth century; a very fine rain was falling, winter was bidding farewell with a drizzle coming down from the heights...

III

Still...